Barker McGee

To Jennifer and Matthew, with love, Dad.
G.E.

To all the Barkers, don't ever give up!
T.R.

Canadian Cataloguing in Publication Data

Elliott, George, 1964-
Barker McGee

ISBN 1-894546-01-6

I. Reid, Thomas II. Title.

PS8559.L5445B37 2000 jC813'.6 C00-900088-7
PZ7.E445Ba 2000

ImaginInk Creations Incorporated
45 Lisgar St., Suite 201
Toronto, Ontario, Canada M6J 3T3

Designed by Glyphics Inc.

Printed and bound in Canada

little thinker books is an imprint of ImaginInk Creations Inc.

Special thanks to Dave Bluestein, Martin Smith and Rob Elliott.

Barker McGee

Written by George Elliott • Illustrated by Thomas Reid

little thinker books

In an old sunken pirate ship deep in the sea,
Off the coast of an island called Skullduggery,

Lived an old dogfish who, after all he'd been through,
Was as tough as the sole of an old leather shoe.

On his back was a scarred-over, crescent-shaped mark
From a brawl with a pugnacious hammerhead shark.

And the gash on his nose and a tooth in his tail
Were from fighting a white shark and black killer-whale.

Barker McGee was the name of this fellow.
He was grumpy and gruff and had eyes bloodshot yellow.

Folks said he ate children if they misbehaved.
And picked his teeth clean with the bones that he saved.

All the fish in the oceans and seas came to fear him.
Even the bravest ones would not go near him.

And so, lonely and bitter, in deep misery,
Barker lived without loved ones or friends in the sea.

Then one day when Barker was moping about
He heard in the distance a desperate shout.

“Help! Help!” cried a little fish, swimming his way.
“Leave me be or I’ll eat you!” Barker barked. “Stay away!”

"Oh p-p-please do not eat me," the little fish said.
"I desperately need you to help me instead!
"I'm Casey McFinn, sir, from Cape Somerset,
And my family and friends have been trapped in a net.

“The net is too strong for my small teeth to chew.
I need someone bigger to help me cut through.”

“Well I won’t!” Barker said. “Leave me be! Go away!
“I don’t want to deal with *your* problems today!”

"But the fishermen are coming! My family will die!
Oh, won't you please help, sir? Please won't you try?

"No one but you can bite through that tough rope.
Don't you see?" Casey cried. ***"You're my very last hope!"***

Barker paled as a memory he'd tried to forget
Filled his heart with a feeling of loss and regret.

"Those were my father's last words!" Barker cried.
"He said those same words on the day that he died.

"I was too young and frightened to help set them free.
It was my fault my family was hauled from the sea."

Barker sniffled and said, with a tear in his eye,
"I **will** help you, Casey. At least I will try."

"Lead the way!" Barker barked, and they swam like two streaks
Over deep sea ravines and immense coral peaks.

As they came to the net, there arose a sad wail.
"Please help us! Please save us! ***We'll die if you fail***!"

Doubt filled Barker's mind.
A chill ran through his core.
"Can I do it?" he wondered.
"I failed once before."

But he grasped the net hard
and he chomped and he slashed
And he chewed and he crunched
and he gnawed and he gnashed.

With all of his strength Barker heaved and he grunted.
But the rope was too tough. Barker's teeth became blunted.

The fish in the net started thrashing and crying,
"Don't let us die here! **Keep trying! Keep trying!**"

"I CAN'T!" Barker shouted. "My teeth can't cut through it. I'm too old and weak. I knew it! I knew it!"

Casey looked straight at Barker and said, "Don't lose hope.
There must be some way you can cut through this rope!"

The fish in the net became still as the sea.
Casey said, "We *believe* in you, Barker McGee."

Barker paused.
He thought hard
for a moment . . . or two.
"Wait just a second.
I know what to do!"

Barker knew that the best hope lay back at his ship.
He turned and swam off at a blistering clip.

On the sea bottom, buried right to its hilt,
In a hundred years build up of sand and sea silt,

Was the saber of someone both hated and feared —
A nasty old pirate named Barton Badbeard!

The handle and scabbard were coated with rust,
A thick, gnarly coating of hard, brittle crust.

Barker frowned at the solid, black, barnacled blob.
"I hope this old saber is up to the job."

He took a firm hold of the hilt with his teeth
Gave a tug and a gleaming blade slid from the sheath.

Barker's heart leapt with hope and he swam at top speed
Over forests of coral and fields of seaweed.

Then he saw high above him
the boat on the water.
It was starting to haul in
its catch for the slaughter.

"This is it! I have only
one chance to cut through it."
Barker clenched his jaw tighter,
"I know I can do it!"

Like a strange, flying swordfish he leaped from the sea.
The blade sliced through the ropes with a "Snick-snicker-snee!"

The trapped fish escaped in a shower of bubbles,
Ecstatic, at last, to be free of their troubles."

"THREE CHEERS!" shouted Casey, "for Barker McGee!
The kindest and bravest dogfish in the sea!"

As they cheered Barker felt himself choke up with pride.
For the first time in years he felt happy inside.

The fishermen left and they never came back
For fear of a Badbeard-the-swordfish attack.

The waters were safe then for many years after,
Abundantly filled with the sounds of fish laughter.

And for the rest of his long life, Barker McGee
Was the happiest dogfish that lived in the sea.